FUNNY BONES

FUNNY BONES

CARTOON MONSTER RIDDLES

by Mike Thaler, the creator of Letterman

LAUREL-LEAF LIBRARY

Published by
Dell Publishing Co., Inc.
1 Dag Hammarskjold Plaza
New York, New York 10017

Laurel-Leaf ® TM 766734, Dell Publishing Co., Inc.

ISBN: 0-440-92616-5

Reprinted by arrangement with Franklin Watts, Inc.
Printed in the United States of America
First Laurel-Leaf printing—October 1978
Second Laurel-Leaf printing—August 1979

THE LAUREL-LEAF LIBRARY brings together under a single im-
print outstanding works of fiction and nonfiction particularly suit-
able for young adult readers, both in and out of the classroom.
The series is under the editorship of Charles F. Reasoner, Profes-
sor of Elementary Education, New York University.

To M.E.M. a GEM

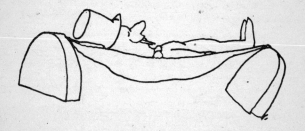

**What is it called when a vampire
gets a lot of nice letters?**

Fang mail.

What does a polite vampire say?

Fang you very much.

What's it called when a vampire kisses you good night?

Necking.

What will chase a vampire away?

Ring around the collar.

What do you call a vampire who buys the Brooklyn Bridge?

A sucker.

What do you call a vampire who stays up all night?

An all-night sucker.

What fruit does a hungry vampire like best?

A nectarine.

Where does a vampire take a bath?

In a bat tub.

What's a vampire's favorite dance?

The vaults.

**What's pink, has a curly tail,
and drinks blood?**

A hampire.

Who has feathers, wings, and fangs?

Count Duckula.

Why is a vampire a cheap date?

He eats necks to nothing.

What animal do vampires like best?

The giraffe.

Where does a vampire save?

At the blood bank.

Where does a traveling vampire stay?

At a mold-tel.

Who is the fastest monster in the world?

Count Dragula.

What does an old vampire call his false teeth?

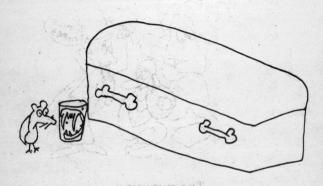

A new-fangled device.

Who referees the monster baseball game?

The vumpire.

Who is the mascot of the monster baseball team?

The bat boy.

What is a favorite game of vampires?

Bat-minton.

Who is a vampire likely to fall in love with?

The girl necks door.

How was Frankenstein's monster made?

From things that were hanging around.

How did Dr. Frankenstein amuse his monster?

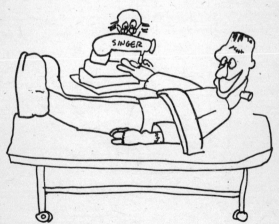

He kept him in stitches.

Why did the monster's girl friend break up with him?

Because he had a crush on her.

Why did the werewolf go to San Francisco?

To bay at the moon.

**What do you call a werewolf in
sheep's clothing?**

A werewoolf.

What does every werewolf suffer from?

Five o'clock shadow.

What kind of wolves hang out at the laundromat?

Wash-and-werewolves.

What did ancient Egyptians call their mothers?

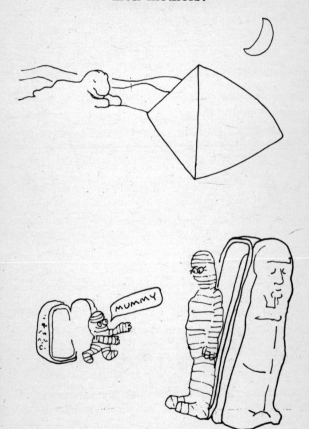

What do you call a person who has sat in a tomb for 2,000 years?

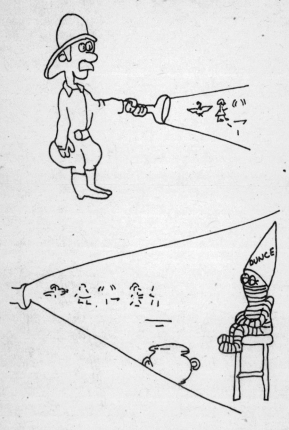

A dummy.

What do you call an ancient Egyptian dance instructor?

Arthur Mummy.

What city has the most witches?

Witchita. He-he-he!

How do witches drink tea?

With cups and sorcerers.

What do you call a witch who goes to the beach but won't go in the water?

A chicken sand witch.

What do witches eat on picnics?

Deviled eggs, deviled ham, and
devil's food cake.

What do you usually get when you eat at a witch's house?

Potluck.

Why do little witches get A's in school?

Because they're good at spelling.

What city has the most ghosts?

Spookane, Washington.

What state has the most ghosts?

OOOOOOOOOOOhio.

What country has the most ghosts?

Ghosta Rica.

What is a ghost's favorite day?

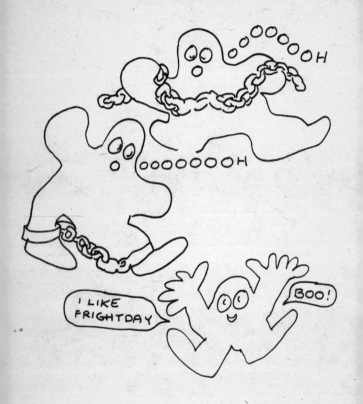

Moanday.

Where do monsters travel on vacation?

From ghost to ghost.

What spirit was a great painter?

Vincent Van Ghost.

What is it called when ghosts star in a big television show?

A spooktacular.

How do you make a ghost float?

With two scoops of vanilla ice cream and a bottle of root beer.

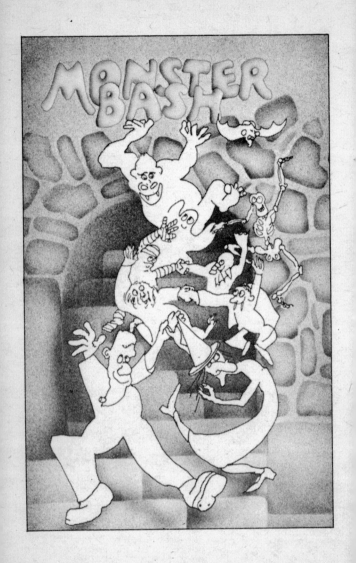

Where do you get a monster degree?

CLASS OF '75

At ghoullege.

Which monster eats the fastest?

The goblin.

What do giants like to eat best?

Home cooking.

What are a giant's favorite vegetables?

Mashed potatoes and squash!

What is a ghoul's favorite dessert?

Yello with whipped scream.

What do ghouls eat for breakfast?

Scream of Wheat.

What does a ghoul order at a delicatessen?

A sa-limy sandwich.

What is the favorite dish of Hungarian demons?

Ghoulash!

Who does a fiend see every Saturday night?

His girl fiend.

Who does a ghoul see every Saturday night?

His ghoul friend.

What position does a monster play on a hockey team?

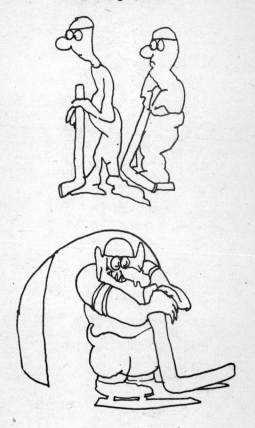

Ghoulie.

What's the monster's favorite baseball team?

The Giants.

What monster was president of France?

Charles de Ghoul.

What ghost was emperor of France?

Napoleon Bones-apart

What is the scariest waterway in America?

The Eerie Canal.

Why did the monster go to the hospital?

To have his ghoul stones removed.

What Chinese monster sneezes the most?

Fu Man-chooooo!

What do you call an overweight monster
who lives at the opera?

The Fat-tum of the Opera.

What kind of bears do ghouls like best?

Pall-bears.

What's it called when demons show off?

A demon-stration.

What kind of horse does the headless horseman ride?

A nightmare.

What game did Dr. Jekyll like to play best?

HERE I COME, READY OR NOT!

Hyde and seek.

What is the favorite story of little ghouls?

Ghoulliver's Travels.

What kind of monster loves boating?

A rowbot.

How do Martians drink tea?

Out of flying saucers.

What is soft, sweet, white, and comes from Mars?

Martian-mallows.

What makes a cemetery very noisy?

The coffin.

How do skeletons eat mashed potatoes?

In gravy.

What monster makes funny noises in its throat?

A gargoyle.

What monster has the best hearing?

The eeriest.

What do you call one-eyed monsters who ride motorcycles together?

Cycle-ops.

What do monsters enjoy most about winter?

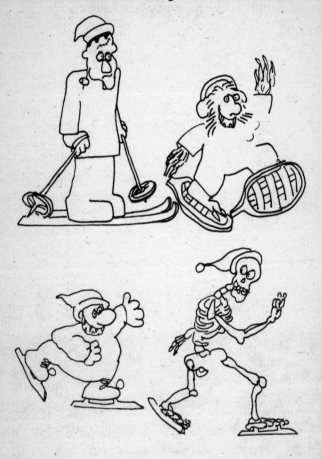

Slay-riding.

What should you do if you meet King Kong?

Give him a big banana.

How does the abominable snowman impress people?

He puts his beast foot forward.

Why are gym teachers never possessed by demons?

Because they exorcise a lot.

What happens to a mummy who eats too many archaeologists?

No, it's a mummy ache.

What do you call a left-handed werewolf pitcher?

A southpaw.

What does King Kong have for lunch?

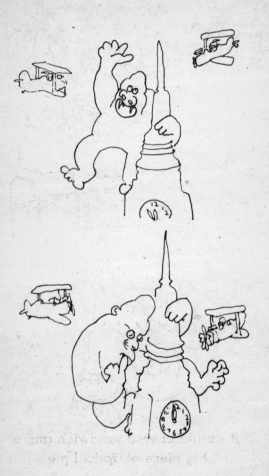

A gorilla cheese sandwich and a big piece of apricot pie.

What do you call a monster that comes down your chimney at Christmas?

Santa Claws.

What's the favorite monster holiday?

Fangsgiving.

ABOUT THE AUTHOR

Mike Thaler was born in Los Angeles and now lives in Stone Ridge, New York. He is a sculptor, draftsman, and song writer. In addition he teaches a writers' workshop and does volunteer work in prisons. Mr. Thaler is presently working on a children's musical. He is the illustrator of William Cole's *Knock Knocks: The Most Ever*, available in a Laurel-Leaf edition.